CORNELIA
and the Jungle Machine

Nora Brech —

CORNELIA
and the Jungle Machine

GECKO PRESS

"I don't want to live here," says Cornelia.

"There's no one to play with."

"*If you're not going to help, go and have a look around outside.*"

"Hi there, I'm Fredrik. I wondered who was moving into the old house."

"*Do you really live here? All by yourself?*" *Cornelia asks.*
"*No, with all my inventions. Want to see them?*"

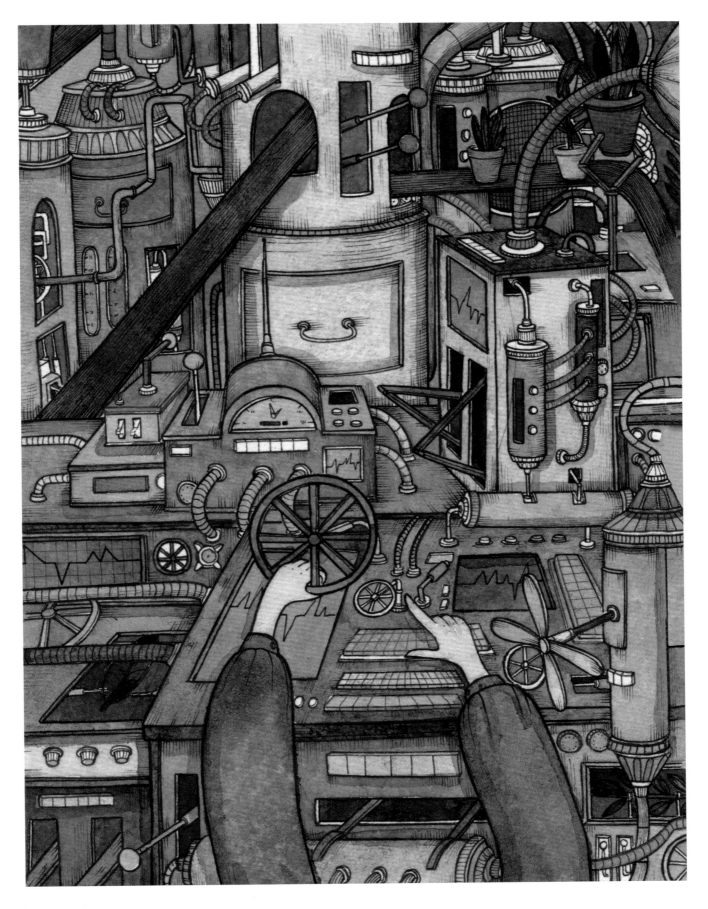

"This one's the best. *A JUNGLE MACHINE*. Hold on tight!"

"See you again tomorrow?" Cornelia asks.
"Every day, if you like," says Fredrik.

"*Let's not tell them. They won't believe us anyway,*"
whispers Cornelia.

"*A walk in the forest seems to have helped,*" says Dad.
What helped is a jungle machine, thinks Cornelia.

This edition first published in 2019 by Gecko Press
PO Box 9335, Wellington 6141, New Zealand
info@geckopress.com

English-language edition © Gecko Press Ltd 2019
Translation © Don Bartlett 2019
Text and illustrations © Nora Brech

First published by H. Aschehoug & Co. (W. Nygaard) As, 2017
Published in agreement with Oslo Literary Agency

This translation has been published with the financial support
of NORLA.

NORLA
NORWEGIAN LITERATURE ABROAD

Edited by Penelope Todd
Typesetting by Tina Delceg
Printed in China by Everbest Printing Co. Ltd, an accredited
ISO 14001 & FSC-certified printer

ISBN hardback 978-1-776572-59-5

For more curiously good books, visit geckopress.com